SCHOLASTIC
Let's Find Out
My REBUS Reader

POP the Bubbles!

by Joan Michael

SCHOLASTIC INC.
New York Toronto London Auckland Sydney New Delhi Hong Kong

I see bubbles in the  .

Pop the bubbles! Pop, pop the bubbles!

I see bubbles in the  drink .

Pop the bubbles! Pop, pop the bubbles!

I see bubbles in the 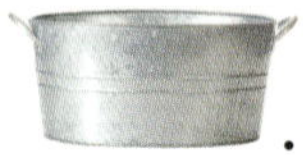 .
tub

Pop the bubbles! Pop, pop the bubbles!

I see bubbles in the  .

ocean

Pop the bubbles! Pop, pop the bubbles!

I see bubbles in the  .

fishbowl

Pop the bubbles! Pop, pop the bubbles!

I see bubbles in the  .
gum

Pop the bubbles! Pop, pop the bubbles!

I see a bubble up close!